tiger tales
5 River Road, Suite 128, Wilton, CT 06897
Published in the United States 2018
Originally published in Great Britain 2018
by Little Tiger Press
Text and illustrations copyright © 2018 Jane Chapman
Visit Jane Chapman at www.ChapmanandWarnes.com
ISBN-13: 978-1-68010-103-4
ISBN-10: 1-68010-103-X
Printed in China
LTP/1400/2193/0218

For more insight and activities,
visit us at www.tigertalesbooks.com

To Susan Beatson, with grateful thanks
- J.C.

Just Like You!

by Jane Chapman

tiger tales

Snowflake was the tiniest, fuzziest mammoth in the herd.
"Sweeter than honey," whispered Mama.
"Brighter than the brightest star," smiled Pops.
And they cuddled her close.

Snowflake soon began to wonder at the huge world around her. "Wow," she gasped, as the mammoth herd traveled through vast icy plains and past towering mountains of ice.

She snuggled up to Mama and Pops
when storms raged and the sky's angry
roars echoed through the mountains.

"You're safe with me, precious,"
whispered Pops, drawing her close.
But Snowflake was afraid.

I'm so tiny, and the world is
enormous, she thought. *When
will I be big like Pops and Mama?*

Pops was Snowflake's hero.
He **toppled** the tallest trees so that
she could nibble on tender shoots.

He **plowed** through snowdrifts so she had room to play.

He even snuffled up snowflakes
and puffed them out
in a cooling **whoosh** of sparkles!

But when Snowflake pushed at the trees, their leaves barely rustled.

When she tried to break through snowdrifts, she needed to be rescued.

And snuffling up snow always ended the same way.

AAAAAACHOOO!

"You light up my day, little one," laughed Pops, ruffling her fur.

"But I don't want to be little," sniffed Snowflake. "I want to be big and strong like you!"

"You will be one day — maybe even bigger," said Pops, "but for now, Mama and I are here to take care of you."

Snowflake sighed.

One day, Pops had an idea.
"There's something special I'd like to
show you, but it's far, far away,"
he smiled. "Do you feel big enough for
a journey? Just the two of us?"
Snowflake squealed with delight.
"An adventure?!"

The next morning, they waved good-bye to
Mama and set off toward the mountains.

"Come on, Pops!"
Snowflake called.
"Try to keep up!"

The sun climbed higher in the sky as Snowflake

hopped and jumped

in Pops's big footprints.

But her skipping turned to
shuffling as the day went on.

Slower . . .

and slower . . .

"Come up here, sweetheart," chuckled Pops,
scooping up Snowflake with his trunk and turning her around.
"I don't want to go back! I want to keep going!"
cried Snowflake. "What about the special something?"

"We're not going home yet," laughed Pops.
"Look at how far you've come . . . ."

Snaking away from the
horizon was a trail of footprints.

"I'm so proud of you," grinned Pops. "That's
a very long walk for a very small mammoth."

Snowflake was amazed that her tiny steps had taken her so far.

Pops trudged onward until the low
sun turned the snow pink.

Rising up before them
was a **huge** tree,
leafless and alone.

"We're here," whispered Pops.
Snowflake was confused.
"But I thought we were coming
to see something special!"
she cried.

Pops slid Snowflake down his trunk.
"Look closer," he smiled.
There on the tree were lines and
swirls etched into the bark.

"Every mark celebrates a
mammoth," said Pops.
"Look, this is me! My mama
measured me up against this
tree when I was the same
age as you are now."

"But you were even smaller
than me!" gasped Snowflake,
tracing the line with her trunk.

Pops took a stick and marked just above Snowflake's head. "Every year we'll come back to this tree and you will see that you've grown a little bit more," he said.

"And every year, you'll see
that you are still **enormous**,
Pops!" giggled Snowflake,
scrambling up to make
a new mark for him.

"Let's go and tell Mama all about our day," said Pops, turning into the wind. Snow whirled around his feet as they began the long journey home.

"I love you, Pops," yawned Snowflake, snuggling into his soft fur. "And one day I'll be **big and strong**, just like you!"